Walt Disney's
Lady and the TRAMP
P9-CCD-660

It was Christmas at Jim Dear and Darling's house. There were so many presents under the tree that Darling didn't know where to start. So Jim Dear handed her a big box.

As soon as Darling untied the ribbon, out jumped a beautiful cocker spaniel puppy.

"Do you like her, Darling?" asked Jim Dear.

"Oh, I love her," Darling answered. "What a perfectly beautiful little lady".

Lady was loved and pampered, and she made friends with the neighbors, Jock the Scottie and Trusty the bloodhound. One day she asked them what it meant that there was going to be a "happy event" at her house.

"It means your mistress is going to have a baby," said Tramp, a scruffy-looking mongrel who was passing by. "Better watch out! When the baby moves in, the dog moves out!" he said.

Sure enough, a baby was born to Jim Dear and Darling. Lady was happy for them.

But before long, things changed for the worse. A lady named Aunt Sarah arrived with her two Siamese cats, Si and Am. She was to look after the baby and Lady while Jim Dear and Darling took a holiday.

The sly cats tried to get at the goldfish and the canary, and they made quite a mess. Lady was trying to stop them when Aunt Sarah came in. She didn't believe her darling cats had done the damage.

"You naughty dog! You'll be punished for this," she said.

Aunt Sarah hauled Lady off to the pet store, and told the owner to put a muzzle on her. Lady had never worn a muzzle, and she was frightened.

So she wriggled out of Aunt Sarah's arms and ran into the street. She didn't care where she went. She just wanted to get away from Aunt Sarah.

As Lady dashed by, a gang of stray dogs saw her and started to chase her. Lady was exhausted by the time they cornered her in a dead-end alley.

"They'll get me now," Lady thought hopelessly.

But at that moment, the mongrel Tramp appeared out of nowhere, snarling at the strays.

As soon as the other dogs saw Tramp, they ran away with their tails between their legs.

Lady was very confused, until Tramp said, "Hi there! Remember me? I could never forget your pretty face. What are you doing in this part of town?"

At that point Lady recognized the mongrel who had visited her neighborhood. She was relieved to find a friend – but the muzzle kept her from talking to Tramp.

The first thing to do was to get the muzzle off so that Lady could speak and eat. Tramp led her to the zoo. "I know someone there who will be able to help," he said.

A beaver gnawed through the strap for Lady. Then he used the muzzle as a log-puller!

Once Lady had the muzzle off, she told Tramp her story.

Tramp knew that Lady was hungry. He took her to a romantic Italian restaurant where he was friendly with the owners. Soon the dogs were eating spaghetti in the moonlight.

In the morning, Tramp started to walk Lady home. But on the way, he decided to chase some chickens. The angry chickens made a racket, and minutes later, their owner came running.

Tramp got away, but Lady was caught and put in the dog pound. The scruffy dogs already there teased her about her fancy collar until she was ready to cry.

Lady was soon taken home. But then she was put outside in a doghouse with a short chain. Jock and Trusty came to visit, but she was so ashamed she could barely speak.

Later, Tramp showed up and acted like nothing had happened. But Lady was furious. "Go away! I don't ever want to see you again!" she snarled.

That night, a rat climbed up a tree next to the house and onto the roof. Lady saw it sneak into the baby's room. She rushed to the end of her chain, barking and nearly choking herself. Tramp, who had stayed nearby, came running.

"A big rat just went into the baby's room," Lady cried.

"Don't worry. I'll get him for you!" Tramp shouted.

As Tramp raced into the house, Lady broke her chain, and they both ran to the baby's room. Tramp grabbed the rat just as it climbed onto the crib.

The noise woke Aunt Sarah and she rushed into the room. When she saw the dogs she was too angry to notice the rat.

"Into the cellar with you!" she cried, pushing Lady with a broom. Then she called the dog pound to pick up Tramp.

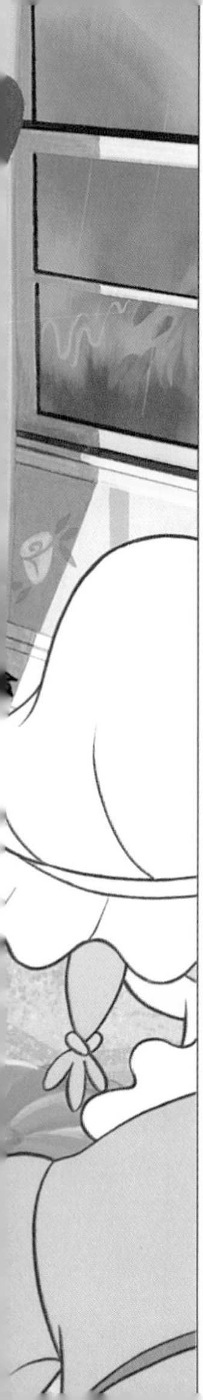

Tramp was being taken away just as Jim Dear and Darling returned. They brought Lady up from the cellar and she showed them the dead rat in the baby's room.

"Oh dear! I thought they were after the baby, but it was a rat!" said Aunt Sarah.

Meanwhile, Trusty and Jock followed the trail of the pound wagon. "We must help him. He may be a mongrel, but he's a good fellow!" they told each other.

When they caught up, Trusty said, "I'll head him off," and ran in front of the pound wagon. The horse reared and the wagon tipped over.

Back at the house, Jim Dear told Lady, "We'll find your friend. He saved our baby's life!" Soon, Lady and Tramp were reunited.

Tramp was given a collar and a license, and he and Lady settled down. He was happy to have a home of his own.

When Christmas came again, there were four mischievous puppies under the tree. Of course, the loyal friends, Jock and Trusty, joined the celebration, too!